For everyone who dares to be different.

ISBN: 978-1-9997628-4-1
First published in the UK, May 2019 by Owlet Press
Text copyright - Samuel Langley-Swain 2019
Illustrations copyright - Ryan Sonderegger 2019

Revised edition, August 2020
Text copyright - Samuel Langley-Swain 2020
Illustrations copyright - Ryan Sonderegger 2020

What Wesley Wore

Samuel Langley-Swain
Ryan Sonderegger

A book about acceptance

First published in the UK
by Owlet Press
www.owletpress.com

In Westburrow Wood, everyone was expected,
to follow the rules - fit in OR be rejected!

But then there was Wesley; he always stood out.
He just didn't get what these 'rules' were about.

The weasels all hated his 'outfits' and 'stuff'.
Why wasn't he 'normal'? They'd all had enough!

So they crafted a plan. Wesley had to be told!
They just couldn't deal with a weasel THAT bold.

As Wesley set off on his walk the next morning,
a crowd of protesters appeared without warning.

Poor Wesley raced home, with his confidence crushed.
The tears started falling – his cheeks became flushed.

As Dad's great advice put a smile on his face,
Wesley put every treasure back into its place.
He picked out the boldest and brightest display
of colourful clothes, his fears fading away.

He strode past the bullies, who'd kicked up a stink.
Not caring this time, what those weasels would think.

"Give me some space."
"I'm getting tired of this place."
"You'll never again take the smile off my face."

And then, all the weasels of Westburrow Wood looked sheepishly over to where Wesley stood.

"Your clothes are so pretty."

"Being stuck here seems a pity."

"Leave this lot behind. You belong in the city!"

As Wesley thought hard, Dad kept watch all along.
New starts would be tough. They both had to be strong.

"Wipe those tears from your face."

"Our love, no one can replace."

"My son, now's your chance, to live your life, find your place."

With one final hug, they whisked Wesley away.
Deep down, Dad knew things would be better this way.

The next day, a sadness spread all through the wood.
This shocked all the weasels, who'd thought they'd feel good.
A letter arrived for all those who'd made fun.
It said 'I forgive you'. They knew what they'd done.

Their mean words and actions drove Wesley away.
Would kindness have helped Wesley feel he should stay?
They met Wesley's Dad, full of guilt, teary-eyed.
In spite of his anger, he showed them inside.

In Wesley's old room, he shared clothes left behind.
Could walking in Wesley's shoes help change their mind?

As they opened their minds to a new point of view,
the weasels felt joy, trying out something new.

The weasels felt special, with a smile on each face,
now that Westburrow Wood was a colourful place.
As Wesley returned from his life in the city,
he loved seeing the welcoming wood look so pretty.

His joy grew each visit and Dad proudly saw
how everyone learned to love what Wesley wore.

OWLET PRESS

Growing into wisdom

Discover even more stories to treasure!

That splashy, magical mermaid, wherever can she be? Join our intrepid family to find out! In this underwater adventure, readers will enjoy trying to find the hiding mermaid, while meeting magical endangered wildlife on the way.

RRP: £7.99

The next time you look up at the night sky, you might see the sparkling metal planet with all its robots and their robo-babies.
A story about all the ways babies arrive into their families like IVF, surrogacy, donors and adoption.

RRP: £7.99

In the 'Polka Dot Pet Shop', where every animal is magical and marvellous, we find a plain, brown mouse who struggles to see how he fits in. Young readers learn about confidence, as the mouse realises his own unique talents.

RRP: £7.99

Follow @owletpress on social media or visit www.owletpress.com to learn more about us.